Star SCENE

CELEB FA[...]

The 411 On All Your Faves

MW00966675

ASHLEY

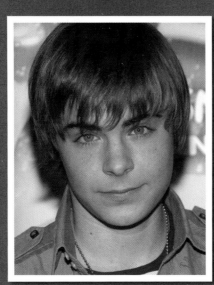

ZAC

HILARY

By Michael Anne Johns

SCHOLASTIC INC.

New York   Toronto   London   Auckland   Sydney
Mexico City   New Delhi   Hong Kong   Buenos Aires

Photo Credits:

Cover:
Corbin Bleu © Michael Tran/FilmMagic.com; Miley Cyrus © Lawrence Lucier/FilmMagic.com; Zac Efron © Michael Tran/FilmMagic.com; Drake Bell © Ralph Notaro/Getty Images; Ashley Tisdale © Chris Daniels/ Retna Ltd.

Page 1: (Left) © Daniel Shapiro / Retna Ltd.; (Center) © Lawrence Lucier/Filmmagic.com; (Right) © Jon Kopaloff/FilmMagic.com; Page 4: © Jeff Kravitz/FilmMagic.com; Page 5: (top) © Lawrence Lucier/FilmMagic. com (bottom) © David Atlas/Retna; Page6: © Michael Tran/FilmMagic.com; page 7: (top) © Daniel Shapiro / Retna Ltd. (bottom) © Michael Tran/FilmMagic.com; page 8: © Sara De Boer / Retna Ltd.; Page 9: (Top) © Jon Kopaloff/FilmMagic.com (Bottom) © Daniel Shapiro/Retna Ltd.; Page 10: ©Michael Tran/FilmMagic.com; Page 11: (Both) ©Michael Tran/FilmMagic.com; Page 12: © Sara De Boer/Retna Ltd.; Page 13: AP Photo/Damian Dovarganes; Page 14: © Carley Margolis/FilmMagic.com; page 15: (top) © Grayson Alexander/Retna Ltd. (Bottom) Michael Loccisano/FilmMagic.com; Page 16: © Mark Sullivan/Wirelmage.com; Page 17: (Both) © Duffy-Marie Arnoult/WireImage.com; Page 18: ©Jon Kopaloff/FilmMagic.com; Page 19: (Top) ©suzan/ allactiondigital/Retna.ltd (Bottom) © Chris Polk/FilmMagic.com; Page 20: ©John Ricard/FilmMagic.com; Page 21: (Top) © Ricard/Retna Ltd. (Bottom) © Michael Tran/ FilmMagic.com; Page 22: AP Photo/Luis Martinez; Page 23: (Top) © Rena Durham/Retna Ltd. (Bottom) AP Photo/Chris Polk; Page 24: © Mark Savage/Corbis; Page 25: (Top) © Sara De Boer/Retna Ltd. (Bottom) © Jason Merritt/FilmMagic.com; Page 26: © John Shearer/WireImage.com; Page 27: (Top) © Jon Kopaloff/FilmMagic.com (Bottom) © David Livingston/Getty Images; Page 28: © Michael Tran/FilmMagic.com; Page 29: Vince Bucci/Getty Images; Page 30: © Jason Merritt/FilmMagic. com; Page 31: (Top) © Paul Smith/ Featureflash/Retna, (Bottom) © Desiree Navarro/FilmMagic.com; Page 32: © Mathew Imaging/FilmMagic.com; Page 33: (Top) © Mathew Imaging/ FilmMagic.com; (Bottom) © Lawrence Lucier/FilmMagic.com; Page 34: © Dale Wilcox/WireImage.com; Page 35: (Top) © Ralph Notaro/Getty Images (Bottom) © Ralph Notaro/Getty Images; Page 36: © Alex Blasquez/Retna Ltd. Page 37: (Top) © Todd Williamson/FilmMagic.com (Bottom) © Jeff Kravitz/FilmMagic.com; Page 38: © Jon Kopaloff/FilmMagic.com; Page 39: (Top) © Marc Morrison / Retna Ltd. (Bottom) © Jason Merritt/FilmMagic.com; Page 40: © Jesse Grant/WireImage.com; Page 41: (Left) © Jeffrey Mayer/ WireImage.com (Right) © Chris Daniels/Retna Ltd.; Page 42: © Jason Kempin/FilmMagic.com; Page 43: © Theo Wargo/ WireImage.com; Page 44: © John Sciulli/ WireImage.com; Page 45: (Top & Bottom) © Dale Wilcox/WireImage.com; Page 46: © Amy Graves/WireImage.com Page 47: (Top) © Chris Polk/ FilmMagic.com (Bottom) © Jeff Kravitz/FilmMagic.com; Page 48: © Jason Merritt/ FilmMagic.com

ISBN-13: 978-0-439-87972-9
ISBN-10: 0-439-87972-8

Copyright © 2006 by Scholastic Inc.

Published by Scholastic Inc. SCHOLASTIC and associated logos are trademarks and/or registered trademarks of Scholastic Inc. All rights reserved.

12 11 10 9 8 7 6 5 4 3 2 1   6 7 8 9 10/0

Designed by Two Red Shoes Design

Printed in the U.S.A.
First printing, November 2006

iNtRO

Are you one of those **"authorities"** who has trivia facts at your fingertips? Especially about your favorite HOTTIES, *teen queens*, **and celebrities in general?**

Or are you one of those fans who devours teen magazines, gossip columns, and entertainment Web sites just for the *latest bits of info* about Jesse McCartney, Dylan and Cole Sprouse, and Zac Efron?

Well, no matter if you are a *know-it-all* or a **WANNA-KNOW-IT-ALL**, **Celeb Fact Files!** is just for you! In it you can find out your favorites' birthdays, hometowns, and favorite fast foods. This little book has **stax and stax of fax** — all fun, fun, FUN.

Check it out and don't be surprised if your friends come to you for the fun stuff about *your faves*.

Zac Efron

Zac Efron, 19, admits he's always known he wanted to act and sing, and got his start in local musical theater in his hometown. He first caught the attention of millions of girls when he costarred with Jesse McCartney in the TV series *Summerland*. Then he took over the hottie title when he starred in the Disney Channel's huge TV movie hit *High School Musical*. Word has it that Zac has been offered several network series, which he is considering, and he will be returning as Troy Bolton in *High School Musical 2*, set to be ready in 2007. Zac has also signed to play Link in the 2007 version of *Hairspray*, starring alongside Amanda Bynes, Haylie Duff, and Queen Latifah.

HEAD-TO-TOE STAX OF FAX

Name: Zachary David Alexander Efron

Birthday: October 18, 1987

Astro Sign: Libra

Birthplace: San Luis Obispo, CA

Hometown: Arroyo Grande, CA

Parents: Mom Starla and dad David

Sibling: Brother Dylan (four years younger)

Height: 5'9"

Weight: 135 lbs

Hair: Brown

Eyes: Blue

Childhood Self-Description: "I loved Ninja Turtles and candy, I was terrified of girls, and I was always singing."

Self-Description at 13: "I loved the theater, improv, getting good grades . . . and was definitely not terrified of girls!"

Pets: Two Australian shepherds named Dreamer and Puppy; one Siamese cat named Simon

First Major Purchase: An electric scooter when he was in the sixth grade. "It bankrupted me!"

Secret Goal: To go skydiving

Biggest Fear: Sharks

College: Zac would like to go either to University of California–Los Angeles to study musical theater or to University of Southern California to study film.

FUN-TASTIC FAVORITES

Sports: Surfing, basketball, baseball, skateboarding

Sports Star: Kobe Bryant

Foods: Sushi

Snacks: Krispy Kreme donuts

Candy: Japanese rice paper candy

Drink: Milk

Home-Cooked Meal: Mac 'n' cheese

Fast Food: Honey-mustard barbecue chicken sandwich from Quiznos

Ice Cream: Cherry Garcia

Childhood Books: *Captain Underpants*, *Goosebumps* series, *Hank the Cow Dog*

Movie: *The Goonies*

TV Shows: *American Idol*, *Survivor*, *Price Is Right*

Cars: Toyota Supra (the one from the movie *The Fast and the Furious*), Infinity G-35

Hobby: Zac is restoring his grandfather's vintage cars – a Delorean and a 1965 Mustang

Collection: Baseball cards

Fashion Accessory: Gucci aviator sunglasses

Bands: Coldplay, the Shins, Postal Service

Singer: Jack Johnson

Dream Girl: Catherine Zeta-Jones

School Subject: English. "There's never one right answer!"

Historical Era: 1940s–1950s. "So I could hang with [movie star/dancer] Gene Kelly."

NOTABLE QUOTABLE

On His Preparation for
High School Musical

"We showed up in Utah two weeks before the movie started shooting and we didn't know why. Little did we know that they had two solid weeks of nine-to-six-o'clock rehearsals planned for us. Long hours of just dance rehearsals and basketball practice and then we worked on scenes. It was like boot camp!"

Corbin Bleu

HEAD-TO-TOE STAX OF FAX

Name: Corbin Bleu

Nickname: Bleuman

Birthday: February 21, 1989

Astro Sign: Pisces

Birthplace: Brooklyn, NY

Hometown: Los Angeles (his family moved there when he was 7)

Parents: David and Martha Bleu

Siblings: Sisters Hunter, Phoenix, and Jag (all younger)

Height: 5' 8$^3/_4$"

Weight: 140 lbs

Hair: Brown

Eyes: Brown

Childhood Self-Description: "Wild Thing!"

Self-Description Now: "Secure with who I am. I march to the beat of my own drum."

Best Advice Given: "The only thing that should really matter to me is what I believe."

Language Studied in School: Spanish

Brooklyn-born Corbin followed in his dad David's footsteps when it came to acting. At the age of two, Corbin appeared in commercials for such products as Life cereal, Bounty, Hasbro, and many others. Besides acting, school, and just being a kid, Corbin added dance classes to his busy schedule and then signed with Ford Modeling Agency and did many national print ads. In 1996 Corbin's family moved to Los Angeles, and Corbin began landing roles in TV and feature films. Corbin was cast in his first lead role in *Catch That Kid*. Next came a lead role in the Discovery Kids series *Flight 29 Down*, but it was *High School Musical* that made Corbin every girl's newest crush!

FUN-TASTIC FAVORITES

Sport: Basketball
TV Shows: *Amazing Race*, *CSI: Miami*
Movies: *Chicago*, *Bad Boys II*
Actor: Johnny Depp
Singer: Prince
Car: Porsche Spider
Food: French fries
Fast Food Restaurant: In-N-Out
Drink: Lemonade
Candy: Twix
Ice Cream: Cake Batter ice cream from Cold Stone Creamery
Article of Clothing: His beat-up leather jacket
Colors: Gold and black
School Subject: Science
Book: *The Great Gatsby* by F. Scott Fitzgerald
Author: J. K. Rowling
Musical or Play: *Wicked*

NOTABLE QUOTABLE
On the Most Important
Quality in Friendships

"Honesty is a really big thing. I feel, in relationships, the ability to talk about anything is a big factor."

Ashley Tisdale

HEAD-TO-TOE STAX OF FAX

Name: Ashley Michelle Tisdale
Birthday: July 2, 1985
Astro Sign: Cancer
Birthplace: Monmouth, NJ
Hometown: Neptune, NJ
Parents: Lisa and Mike Tisdale
Sister: Jennifer (older)
Pet: Maltipoo (combination of Maltese and poodle) named Blondie
Height: 5'3"
Weight: 100 lbs
Hair: Blond
Eyes: Brown
Childhood Self-Description: "Funny, always wanted to be the center of attention, and loved to entertain"
Self-Description Now: "More sure of myself. I know who I am and I know where I want to be. I am very focused."
Language Studied in School: Spanish

Born in Monmouth, New Jersey, Ashley was discovered when she was three years old by a talent manager, Bill Perlman, who saw her with her mom, Lisa, in a mall. Perlman had a good instinct and signed the young toddler. Ashley landed a job on her first audition and went on to appear in more than 100 national commercials. When she was eight years old, Ashley won the lead role in the Broadway superhit *Les Misérables*, and then toured with *Annie*. When the Tisdales moved to Los Angeles, Ashley took TV land by storm, guesting or having recurring roles in series such as *Nathan's Choice*, *George Lopez*, *Still Standing*, and more. In 2005 Ashley was cast as Maddie Fitzpatrick in the Disney Channel's *The Suite Life of Zack and Cody*. When the producers for *High School Musical* were looking for a perfect Sharpay, all they had to do was look on their own lot and pick out Ashley!

FUN-TASTIC FAVORITES

Sport: Basketball
TV Shows: *Laguna Beach*, *Surface*
Movie: *My Best Friend's Wedding*
Actresses: Brittany Murphy, Julia Roberts
Singer: Billy Joel
Car: Range Rover
Food: Sushi
Fast Food Restaurant: McDonald's
Drink: Vanilla Ice Blend from Coffee Bean
Candy: Red Swedish Fish
Ice Cream: Cookie Dough
After-School Snack: Cheetos
Fashion Designer/Label: Bebe
Piece of Jewelry: Tiffany necklace
Color: Pink
School Subject: Creative Writing
Book: *The Great Gatsby* by F. Scott Fitzgerald

NOTABLE QUOTABLE

On Her *High School Musical* Experience

"You have no idea how much fun we had. We all stayed at the same hotel, Little America, in Salt Lake City, Utah. We all hung out. It was great to be with everybody I love and adore and singing and dancing every day."

Vanessa Anne Hudgens

HEAD-TO-TOE STAX OF FAX

Name: Vanessa Anne Hudgens
Sometimes Stage Name: Vanessa Anne Hutchinson
Birthday: December 14, 1988
Astro Sign: Sagittarius
Birthplace: Salinas, CA
Hometown: Salinas, CA
Parents: Mom Gina and dad Greg
Sibling: Sister Stella (younger)
Pets: One poodle named Shadow, a bunny, turtles, and fish
First Major Purchase: A limited edition Dior purse
Dream Experience: To go skydiving

Born in Salinas, California, Vanessa began her acting career when she was eight years old and participated in local community theater musicals. She played roles in *Evita, Carousel, The Wizard of Oz, The King and I,* and many more. She loved every minute of it, and soon her family was sure this was what the future held for their eldest daughter. The family moved closer to Los Angeles, as Vanessa's roles grew and grew. Her first feature film was *Thirteen* and then she had a lead in the action-adventure film *Thunderbirds.* But Vanessa always wanted to get back to the first love of her life, so when she was offered the role of Gabriella Montez in the Disney Channel's production of *High School Musical,* she quickly signed on the dotted line. Good move!

FUN-TASTIC FAVORITES

Actresses: The late Natalie Wood, Charlize Theron
Actor: Matt Damon
Clothes: Frankie B jeans
Clothing Style: Vintage
Sports Shoes: Nike
Car: Porsche Carerra GT
Pastime: Shopping
Fitness Routine: Going to the gym and running
Guilty Pleasure: Chocolate
Dinner: BBQ steak or sushi
Fast Food Restaurant: In-N-Out
Cartoon: *SpongeBob SquarePants*
Broadway Musicals: *Phantom of the Opera, Gypsy*

NOTABLE QUOTABLE

On Her *High School Musical* Embarrassing Moment

"It's not so embarrassing, but just so funny. There is a line in the movie where I see Troy for the first time in school. I tell him my mom's company transferred her here from Albuquerque, and for some reason I could not say that line. I would get so tongue-twisted, it was so funny. I watch the scene now and I have no idea why it was so hard for me then!"

GET IN TOUCH WITH ZAC, VANESSA, CORBIN & ASHLEY

Zac Efron,
Corbin Bleu, Ashley Tisdale,
Vanessa Anne Hudgens
c/o *High School Musical*
Disney Channel
3800 West Alameda Avenue
Burbank, CA 91505

Jesse McCartney

The eldest of three children of Ginger and Scot McCartney, Jesse McCartney grew up in suburbs not too far from New York City. He always seemed to know he wanted to perform, and when he was still in elementary school, Jesse was appearing on and off Broadway. He toured with the musical *The King and I,* in which he played Louis. When he was 12 years old, Jesse joined a singing group called the Sugar Beats and then went on to the boy band Dream Street. The group reached pop success but broke up in 2002, and Jesse went on as a solo performer — both as a singer and an actor. By 2004 Jesse released his soon-to-be multiplatinum CD *Beautiful Soul* and was signed to star in the WB Network TV series *Summerland.* Millions of fans later, Jesse is working on his second CD and a new movie and is reading all the fan letters he receives each day!

HEAD-TO-TOE STAX OF FAX

Name: Jesse Abraham Arthur McCartney

Nicknames: Jmac, Jester

Birthday: April 9, 1987

Astro Sign: Aries

Birthplace: New York, NY

Childhood Home: Irvington, NY

Parents: Ginger and Scot McCartney

Siblings: Sister Lea (younger), brother Timmy (younger)

Hair: Blond

Eyes: Blue-green

Scar: A scar on his left eyebrow — he got it when he fell when he was 4 years old.

Pet: A cat named Oliver

Sports Teams: Played JV baseball on his high school team, the Panthers — he's a pitcher and also plays shortstop.

College: Jesse would like to attend UCLA to study film.

Musical Influences: Stevie Wonder, Marvin Gaye, Sting, Babyface, Craig David, Daniel Bedingfield

Instrument: Jesse played the saxophone in his middle school band.

Worst Habits: Jesse claims he can be lazy; bites his nails

Charity: St. Jude's Hospital

"I have a hard time waking up. No alarm clock works! It sounds childish, but I seriously have my manager, my mom, or a buddy of mine wake me up if I have to be somewhere. It's a serious issue! I've been very late for some serious gigs because of it!"

GET IN TOUCH WITH JESSE

Jesse McCartney
c/o Hollywood Records
331 North Maple Drive
Suite 300
Beverly Hills, CA 90210

FUN-TASTIC FAVORITES

Breakfast Food: Scrambled eggs, pumpkin pie

Food: Sushi – California rolls

Meal: His dad's barbecue

Ice Cream: Chocolate

Candy: Gummi Bears, Sour Patch Kids, raspberry Tootsie Roll Pops

Fast Food Restaurant: Wendy's – he loves taco salad and chicken nuggets; in L.A., it's In-N-Out burgers

TV Show: *Friends*

Movies: *Sixth Sense, Grease, American History X, The Italian Job*

Actors: Will Smith, Robin Williams, Jim Carrey

Actresses: Reese Witherspoon, Kate Hudson, Penelope Cruz

Musical Artists: Mario, James Taylor, John Mayer, Jason Mraz, Justin Timberlake

Color: Orange

School Subject: Spanish

Books: *Death Be Not Proud* by John Gunther and *The Great Gatsby* by F. Scott Fitzgerald

Childhood Books: *The Hardy Boys* series

Sports: Baseball, water-skiing, Rollerblading

Sports Teams: New York Yankees and New York Giants

Relaxation: Sleeping

Jamie Lynn Spears

HEAD-TO-TOE STAX OF FAX

Name: Jamie Lynn Marie Spears
Nickname: J Lynn
Birthday: April 4, 1991
Astro Sign: Aries
Birthplace: McComb, MS
Childhood Home: Kentwood, LA
Parents: Lynne and Jamie Spears
Siblings: Sister Britney (older), brother Bryan (older)
Hair: Blond
Eyes: Blue
Height: 5'7"
School: Parklane Academy in McComb, MS
Team Member: Jamie Lynn plays on Parklane's basketball team
Pets: Three Rottweilers named Cane, Spotty, and Sebastian; a teacup poodle named Lady; a German shepherd; two Shih tzu terriers named Mitzi and Bitzi; a Pomeranian named Izzy; a Maltese named Ally; a Yorkie named Beau
College: Jamie wants to go to Louisiana State University.
Instrument: Jamie is learning how to play the guitar.
Worst Habit: Biting her nails

Jamie Lynn Spears is the third and youngest child of Lynne and Jamie Spears. As a little girl, Jamie watched older sister Britney explode onto the entertainment scene from Broadway to the *New Mickey Mouse Club* to becoming the teen queen of song! Though Britney claims that Jamie has a better singing voice than she does, the younger Spears wants to establish herself as an actress, and maybe later she will take on the music industry. Jamie's first onscreen role was in Britney's debut movie *Crossroads*, but since then Jamie has been flying solo. Her Nickelodeon TV series *Zoey 101* is one of the most popular with kids, and she is reading over movie scripts as you read this!

GET IN TOUCH WITH JAMIE

Jamie Lynn Spears
c/o Nickelodeon
Zoey 101
2600 Colorado Avenue
Santa Monica, CA 90404

NOTABLE QUOTABLE
On Getting a Role

"No one is going to cast me just because I have a famous sister. I'll get the job only if I'm the best person who shows up to the audition."

FUN-TASTIC FAVORITES

Sports: Gymnastics, cheerleading, basketball, softball

School Subjects: English, History

Collection: Porcelain dolls

Shoes: Puma, Birkenstock, flip-flops

Jeans: Taunt —"They mysteriously make my legs inches longer. They come in really cool washes and fit so well."

Cartoon Series: *SpongeBob SquarePants*

Singers: Tim McGraw, Kelly Clarkson, Avril Lavigne, and, of course, Britney Spears

Actors: Brad Pitt, Ashton Kutcher, Chad Michael Murray

Food: Caesar salad

Fast Food: Chicken fingers

Hangout: Home — watching scary movies with her girlfriends

Vacation Spot: Nevis in the West Indies

Color: Pink

Lip Gloss: Lancôme Juicy Tubes

Pastime: Shopping

Dylan & Cole Sprouse

Identical twins Dylan and Cole Sprouse were born in Arezzo, Italy, and though they grew up in California, they still hold passports from both the U.S. and Italy. Their grandmother, Jonine Booth Wright, is an actress and drama coach, and she recognized talent in her two little tyke grandsons. She suggested they try their hand at acting, and they shot right out of the starting gate! Both Dylan and Cole shared acting "duties" on the ABC series *Grace Under Fire* for their first professional role. "We were just dribblers then," laughs Dylan. Well, they've come a long way since then and are quickly turning their success on the Disney Channel's hit series *The Suite Life of Zack and Cody* into a showbiz empire. In late 2005, the Sprouse twins signed with Mary-Kate and Ashley Olsen's media company, Dualstar, which will create products and trends centered on Dylan and Cole. It's hoped that the two boys will reach mega-success just like Mary-Kate and Ashley.

NOTABLE QUOTABLE
Dylan on Cole

"He is actually pretty loud. He's really active all the time. . . . He wants to have a good time all the time and he's just fun to be around, but he can also be a little annoying sometimes. [laughs]"

GET IN TOUCH WITH DYLAN & COLE

Dylan and Cole Sprouse
c/o Disney Channel
Suite Life of Zack and Cody
3800 West Alameda Avenue
Burbank, CA 91505

DYLAN & COLE HEAD-TO-TOE STAX OF FAX

Birthday: August 4, 1992

Astro Sign: Leo

Birthplace: Arezzo, Italy

Childhood Home: Southern California

Parents: Matthew and Melanie Sprouse

Siblings: Each other! (Dylan is 15 minutes older than Cole.)

Identifying Marks: Dylan has freckles—and a birthmark his family calls "the angel kiss." Cole has a mole on his chin.

Hair: Blond

Eyes: Green-Blue

Pets: A bulldog named Bubba

NOTABLE QUOTABLE

Cole on Dylan

"He's cool. He's relaxed. He wants to go to bed all the time. [laughs] He really enjoys getting into something like collecting and once he has a goal, he will go for it."

FUN-TASTIC FAVORITES

Name: Dylan Thomas Sprouse

Nickname: Spounge, Dyl

Sports: Snowboarding, surfing, basketball, motocross

Sports Team: Los Angeles Lakers

School Subjects: Science, English, Art

Music: Sum 41, Poison, Nelly, Shakira

Candy: Japanese gummy candies

Pizza: Pepperoni

Dessert: Chocolate chip ice cream

Pastime: Bowling, movies, reading comic books, drawing

FUN-TASTIC FAVORITES

Name: Cole Mitchell Sprouse

Nickname: Coley moley

Sports Team: Utah Jazz

School Subjects: Math, Science, and History

Music: Ja Rule, Missy Elliott, Eminem, Shakira

Colors: Black and blue

Cereal: Frosted Mini Wheats

Dessert: Cake Batter ice cream from Cold Stone Creamery

Actor: Johnny Depp

Pastime: Bowling, going to the movies

Hilary Duff

HEAD-TO-TOE STAX OF FAX

Name: Hilary Ann Lisa Duff
Stage Name: Hilary Duff (sometimes Hilary Erhard Duff)
Nicknames: Hil, Juicy
Birthday: September 28, 1987
Astro Sign: Libra
Birthplace: Houston, TX
Childhood Home: Houston, TX
Parents: Bob and Susan Duff
Sister: Haylie (older)
Boyfriend: Joel Madden of Good Charlotte
Best Friend: Sister Haylie
Height: 5'5"
Hair: Blond
Natural Hair Color: Brown
Eyes: Hazel
Pets: A border collie named Remington; a Chihuahua named Lola; and a mixed-breed named Li'l Dog
Charity: Kids with a Cause

Hilary has been entertaining ever since she was a toddler. By the age of 6, she was traveling with the Cechetti ballet group. Sister Haylie was also in the dance troupe. But even back then, Hilary wanted to act, and she started her career with a small role in the TV miniseries *True Women*. She landed leads in several other TV movies, but her true claim to fame was playing the lead in the hit Disney Channel series *Lizzie McGuire*. More TV movies and feature films followed, along with multiplatinum CDs. By the time Hilary was 16, she was already a full-fledged superstar!

FUN-TASTIC FAVORITES

Sports: Basketball

TV Shows: *Seventh Heaven, Gilmore Girls, Friends*

Movies: *Drop Dead Gorgeous, Ace Ventura, Pet Detective, Romy and Michele's High School Reunion*

Actor: Leonardo DiCaprio

Actress: Cameron Diaz

Singers: Rob Thomas, Steven Tyler

Bands: Good Charlotte, Rancid, AFI, the Postal Service, the Clash, Bloc Party, Muse, Weezer

Car: Range Rover

Food: Sushi, pizza, soul food

Fast Food Restaurant: In-N-Out (burgers!)

Candy: Jolly Ranchers – sour apple

Snack: Pickles

Guilty Pleasure: French fries

Gum: Juicy Fruit

NOTABLE QUOTABLE
On Shopping

"I love clothes. I can't control myself. I have a huge fetish for shoes and clothes and makeup. I'm the kind of person who doesn't like to wear things over and over again."

GET IN TOUCH WITH HILARY

Hilary Duff
c/o Hollywood Records
331 North Maple Drive
Suite 300
Beverly Hills, CA 90210

Romeo

HEAD-TO-TOE STAX OF FAX

Name: Percy Romeo Miller Jr.

Stage Name: Lil' Romeo, Romeo

Nickname: Rome, Romie

Secret Nickname: Leo —"I tell [people] to call me Leo. That's my secret name. Leo's my birth sign, and the lion's my favorite animal."

Birthday: August 19, 1989

Astro Sign: Leo

Birthplace: New Orleans, LA

Current Residences: New Orleans, LA; Houston, TX

Parents: Mom Sonja and dad Master P

Siblings: Two brothers, three sisters (all younger)

Pets: A white terrier name Dollar, a parakeet named Purty

Hair: Brown

Eyes: Brown

Height: 5'11"

Hometown School: St. Luke's Episcopal School in Baton Rouge, LA

Basketball Team: No Limit Ballers

Basketball Position: Point Guard

Romeo is the eldest son of Master P, who is one of the most successful rappers/businessmen in the music industry. But Romeo didn't get where he is today just because of family ties. Oh, no! Way back when Romeo was still a little shorty, he started making his own beats in his dad's home studio. One day, when Master P got home from a concert tour, Romeo played his latest mix. Impressed with his son's talent, Master P encouraged him to work hard on his music. Sometimes Romeo joined his dad on stage and broke out a beat. Romeo's first CD, *Lil' Romeo*, went multiplatinum, and the debut single "My Baby" zoomed up the charts and flew off the store racks. When he was 14, Romeo joined the Nickelodeon Network family with his own series, *Romeo!*, in which he costars with dad Master P. The sky's the limit ever since.

GET IN TOUCH WITH ROMEO

Romeo
c/o Nickelodeon
Romeo!
2600 Colorado Avenue
Santa Monica, CA 90404

FUN-TASTIC FAVORITES

Sports: Basketball, football

Sports Team: Los Angeles Lakers

Sports Stars: Michael Jordan, Kobe Bryant, Shaquille O'Neal, Allen Iverson

School Subjects: Math, English

Hip-Hoppers: Master P, Lil' Bow Wow, Nelly, Eve

Singers: Mya, Alicia Keys

Childhood Book: *Johnny Long Legs* by Matt Christopher

Food: Pizza

Fast Food Restaurant: McDonald's

Breakfast: McDonald's Bacon, Egg, and Cheese Biscuit

Ice Cream: Pralines and cream, butter rum

Home-Cooked Meal: Macaroni and cheese

Cars: Lamborghini, Mercedes Benz, Ferrari

Cartoon Character: Bugs Bunny

Vacation Place: Hawaii

Emma Roberts

HEAD-TO-TOE STAX OF FAX

Name: Emma Roberts
Birthday: February 10, 1991
Astro Sign: Aquarius
Birthplace: Los Angeles, CA
Hometown: Los Angeles, CA
Parents: Eric Roberts and Kelly Cunningham
Sister: Grace (younger)
Famous Relative: Aunt – Julia Roberts
Pet: A cat named Coco Chanel
Hair: Brown
Eyes: Brown
Middle School: Archer School for Girls (Los Angeles) – Emma is now home-schooled.
Instrument: Guitar (She has played since she was 10.)
First Song Learned on Guitar: "Who Will Save Your Soul" by Jewel
Musical Influences: Michelle Branch, Hilary Duff, Skye Sweetnum
Weekly Allowance: $20
Early Ambitions: To be a fashion designer or actress
Celebrity Crush: Singer Teddy Geiger

Born to Hollywood royalty — Emma's dad is actor Eric Roberts and her aunt is Julia Roberts — acting would seem a natural career choice for the 15-year-old. And it was. Though her mom, Kelly Cunningham, didn't want to introduce little Emma to the rough-n-tough grind of Hollywood too early, she did allow Emma to audition for the Johnny Depp movie *Blow*. The then 10-year-old Emma won the role . . . and a star was born. However, until recently, Emma had never seen the entire movie, because *Blow* is rated R!

"The 1950s, because everything was so simple and they got to wear cute fashions. It seemed like a fun time."

FUN-TASTIC FAVORITES

Sports: Swimming and volleyball

Actors: Johnny Depp, Tate Donovan

Actresses: Kirsten Dunst, Rachel McAdams, and Reese Witherspoon

Movies: *The Notebook* and *Just Friends*

TV Shows: *America's Next Top Model*, *The O.C.*, *The Brady Bunch*

Music Groups: The Veronicas –"They are my favorite new band!"– and Aly & A.J.

Singers: Usher, Teddy Geiger, Jesse McCartney, JoJo, Ashlee Simpson

Song on *Unfabulous and More* CD: "I Wanna Be"

Food: Plain cheese pizza

Candy: Dark chocolate Milky Way

Fast Food Restaurant: In-N-Out

Drink: "The new Vanilla Coke kissed by black cherry"

City: New York (especially for shopping)

Pastimes: Shopping for clothes – Emma would love to go to London just to shop! – and reading

School Subject: English

Books: *Gossip Girl* series and *The Clique* series

Author: Meg Cabot, who wrote *The Princess Diaries*

Fashion Designer: Marc Jacobs

Piece of Clothing: Brown zip-up Uggs

Collections: Purses and cosmetics

Car: Range Rover (pink)

Animal: Dog

GET IN TOUCH WITH EMMA

Emma Roberts
c/o Nickelodeon
Unfabulous
2600 Colorado Avenue
Santa Monica, CA 90404

Devon Werkheiser

HEAD-TO-TOE STAX OF FAX

Name: Devon Werkheiser
Birthday: March 8, 1991
Astro Sign: Pisces
Birthplace: Atlanta, GA
Hometown: Atlanta, GA, suburbs
Parents: Gary and Valerie Werkheiser
Sister: Vanessa (older)
Childhood Pet: A dog named Bubba
Hair: Brown
Eyes: Blue
Height: 5'4"
Weight: 104 lbs
Childhood Self-Description: "I cried for the first two years of my life. I was cute, wild, a little mischievous, and funny."
His Middle School: River Trail Middle School in Duluth, GA
Language Studied in School: Spanish
Instrument: Guitar

When Atlanta-born Devon Werkheiser started doing Jim Carrey impressions at the age of six, his parents knew he was meant for more than just entertaining family and friends. He started taking acting classes at Atlanta's Talent Factory and appeared in many community theater productions. Devon's first major showbiz move was when he was 10 years old and he appeared in an NBA commercial with basketball legend Charles Barkley. Shortly after, he played Mel Gibson's young son in *We Were Soldiers*, and he's been working nonstop ever since! Of course tweens and teens know him best for his role as Ned Bigby on Nickelodeon's series *Ned's Declassified School Survival Guide*.

FUN-TASTIC FAVORITES

Sports: Ice hockey
TV Shows: *Fairly Odd Parents*, *24*, *Survivor*
Movies: *Pirates of the Caribbean*, *Lord of the Rings* trilogy, *Harry Potter* films
Actors: Mel Gibson, Jim Carrey, Robin Williams, Mike Myers, Johnny Depp
Actress: Keira Knightley
Car: Aston Martin Vanquish or Ferrari 360 Spyder
Food: Pasta, spicy buffalo wings
Fast Food: Wendy's spicy chicken sandwich or junior bacon cheeseburger
Soda: Root beer
Candy: Sour Patch Kids, Kit Kats, Snickers
Ice Cream: Mint chocolate chip
Piece of Jewelry: Fossil watch
Color: Blue
Book: *Harry Potter* series
Author: J. K. Rowling
School Subject: Social studies
Board Game: Monopoly

NOTABLE QUOTABLE

On His Favorite *Ned's Declassified* Episode

" 'Daydreams' because in that one I got to wear a tux and got to act like James Bond, drive a Mercedes around the school — not really drive. We had grips push us. But it was really fun and the episode turned out to be great."

Lindsey Shaw

HEAD-TO-TOE STAX OF FAX

Name: Lindsey Shaw
Birthday: May 10, 1989
Astro Sign: Taurus
Birthplace: Lincoln, NB
Current Residence: Los Angeles, CA
Parents: Mom Barb
Middle School: St. Francis Xavier in Burbank, CA
High School: Notre Dame, Los Angeles, CA
Acting School: The Jeremiah Comey Film Acting Studios
First Professional Job: A radio spot for the U.S. Tennis Open
Self-Description: "I am a people person."
Biggest Fear: "The ocean and the squishy things in it!"
Dream Experience: To join the Peace Corps

Lindsey began her acting career in grade school plays, and when her family moved from Nebraska to Kansas to Texas to New York to California, she never lost sight of her dream. When she was in New York, 11-year-old Lindsey did the audition and print ads bit, but soon Hollywood called! She had signed with a manager and an agent and was taking acting classes when she landed her first big break, playing Moze on *Ned's Declassified*. . . .

FUN-TASTIC FAVORITES

Sports Team: University of Nebraska Cornhuskers

Sports: Volleyball, softball, swimming, tennis, karate, roller-skating, badminton –"Like Moze, I'm a bit of a tomboy."

School Subject: English

Pastime: Reading

Books: *Where the Red Fern Grows*, *Of Mice and Men*

Authors: John Steinbeck and John Grisham

Childhood Book Series: *Berenstain Bears*

Singer: Jack Johnson

Bands: Coheed and Cambria, Death Cab For Cutie, Gratitude, Maroon 5, Evanescence

Movie: *The Hot Chick*

TV Show: *Charmed*

Jewelry: Earrings

Food: Steak

Fast Food Restaurant: Arby's

Vacation Spot: New York City

NOTABLE QUOTABLE

On the Importance of Education

"Middle school was amazing and a blast. I had awesome teachers and great friends. Schoolwork is a definite priority for me."

Daniel Curtis Lee

HEAD-TO-TOE STAX OF FAX

Name: Daniel Curtis Lee

Nickname: Coast to Coast – His dad gave it to him "because I rule from coast to coast!"

Birthday: May 17, 1991

Astro Sign: Taurus

Birthplace: Clinton, MS

Hometown: Clinton, MS

Current Residence: Long Beach, CA

Parents: Nathaniel Sr. and Sharial C. Lee

Siblings: Sister Yolande (older), brother Nathaniel Jr. (older)

Self-Description: "Curious and rough because I love football. I want to know everything that's going on."

Instruments: Drums and guitar

Daniel's older brother is also an actor — Nathaniel Lee Jr. — so it wasn't surprising when at the age of seven Daniel said he wanted to try his hand at showbiz! That was still back in their hometown of Clinton, Mississippi, but three years later, Daniel was in Hollywood and starring in his first feature film, *Friday After Next.* Always drawn to comedies, Daniel found himself guesting on a number of sitcoms. But he truly found his "perfect" role in Cookie on *Ned's Declassified. . . .*

FUN-TASTIC FAVORITES

Sports: Football, baseball
TV Shows: *Ned's Declassified School Survival Guide*, *Family Guy*, *The Simpsons*
Actor: Jim Carrey
Actress: Mo' Nique
Singer: Andre 3000 (OutKast)
Food: Pizza and fried chicken
Fast Food: McDonald's hamburgers
Drink: V8
Candy: Snickers
Gum: Juicy Fruit
Color: Green
School Subjects: English, History
Pastime: Writing stories
Book: *Holes*
Author: Louis Sachar
Board Game: Monopoly

NOTABLE QUOTABLE

On His *Ned's Declassified* Character . . . Cookie

"My favorite part about Cookie would have to be because he is so lovable. Everyone likes him. He is just crazy and kooky and always getting into trouble."

GET IN TOUCH WITH DEVON, LINDSEY & DANIEL

Devon Werkheiser
Lindsey Shaw
Daniel Curtis Lee
c/o Nickelodeon
Ned's Declassified School Survival Guide
2600 Colorado Avenue
Santa Monica, CA
90404

Sara Paxton

HEAD-TO-TOE STAX OF FAX

Name: Sara Paxton

Nickname: Loxoid – Her best friend gave it to her and it's an inside joke meaning "I tell bad jokes."

Birthday: April 25, 1988

Astro Sign: Taurus

Birthplace: Van Nuys, CA

Childhood Home: Woodland Hills, CA

Parents: Lucia and Steve Paxton

Hair: Blond

Eyes: Green

Height: 5'6"

Weight: 108 lbs

Pet: A sheltie dog named Jenny

First Professional Job: A Coca-Cola commercial when she was six and a half

Second Language: Spanish

Instrument: Flute

Other Talent: Dancing

Early Ambition: To be a veterinarian

College: Hopes to go to University of Southern California and study film.

Sara began her career at age six when she appeared in a Coca-Cola commercial, and she's been going strong ever since. The California-born-'n'-bred girl guested in series such as *Malcolm in the Middle, Will & Grace, Lizzie McGuire, Summerland, Frasier,* and many others. In 2005 Sara won the lead role in the Discovery Kids series *Darcy's Wild Life.* She has appeared in more than a dozen feature films and played the perfect "mean" girl in the hit film *Sleepover.* In the spring of 2006, Sara had the lead role in the teen funflick *Aquamarine.* And also in 2006, Sara is expected to show off her other talent — singing — and is to release her debut CD!

NOTABLE QUOTABLE
On When She First Knew
She Wanted to Perform

"My first memory of loving the limelight was when I was five years old. I used to model for my aunt's children's clothing store, and I loved the applause from the audience."

FUN-TASTIC FAVORITES

Comedienne: Lucille Ball

Actors: Jim Carrey, Ryan Gosling, Orlando Bloom, Kurt Russell

Actresses: Goldie Hawn, Reese Witherspoon

TV Shows: SNL, The O.C., Medium, Grey's Anatomy, I Love Lucy

Movie: The Notebook, Some Like It Hot, Miss Congeniality, Anchorman, Zoolander

Singers: Faith Hill, Pink, Kelly Clarkson

Bands: Rolling Stones, Maroon 5, All American Rejects

Home-Cooked Meal: Her mom's enchiladas with green sauce

Food: Italian and Mexican

Drink: Coca-Cola or juice

Fast Food Restaurant: In-N-Out and McDonald's

Colors: Green, white, gray, black

Board Game: Scrabble

Cartoon: SpongeBob SquarePants

Books: Harry Potter series

Author: Jane Austen (Sara especially loves Pride and Prejudice.)

School Subjects: English and History

Item of Clothing: Her Fendi Spy bag

Car: Range Rover

Vacation Spot: Winter – Mammoth for skiing; Summer – Maui

Sports: Surfing

GET IN TOUCH WITH SARA

Sara Paxton
c/o Aquamarine
20th Century Fox
Home Entertainment
2121 Avenue of the Stars
Los Angeles, CA 90067

Raven-Symoné

HEAD-TO-TOE STAX OF FAX

Name: Raven-Symoné Christina Pearman

Stage Names: Raven, Raven-Symoné

Nickname: Rae, Rave

Birthday: December 10, 1985

Astro Sign: Sagittarius

Birthplace: Atlanta, GA

Parents: Christopher and Lydia Pearman

Brother: Blaize (younger) — he is age 14 and 6' tall and plays basketball for the AAU.

Hair: Dark brown

Eyes: Brown

Height: 5'6"

Pets: A Yorkie dog named Dr. Doolittle; a dog named Czar; a bird named Zeus

High School: North Springs High School in Atlanta, GA

Trademark Motto: "This is a serious situation."

Self-Description: "I am the same person I was when I was in school: crazy and fun."

Personal Style: "Classy and I don't do trendy."

Charities: Make-A-Wish Foundation, Partnership Against Child Abuse, National Safe Kids Campaign

America first fell in love with Raven when, at the age of three, she appeared as Olivia on *The Cosby Show*. Her career suddenly took the fast track, and she starred in TV series such as *Hangin' with Mr. Cooper* and in films such as *The Little Rascals* and *Dr. Doolittle* and *Dr. Doolittle 2*. Along the way — when she was only eight years old — she told her dad she wanted to sing, and the result was her first CD, *Here's to New Dreams*. MCA Records released the CD. Raven was the youngest artist ever signed by them. That was just the beginning. Today Raven stars in one of TV's top-rated sitcoms, *That's So Raven*, is still singing and appearing in movies, and is a producer of *That's So Raven*. She also has released a That's So Raven fragrance and cosmetic collection, heads up a Raven clothing line, is working on a cookbook, and more!

FUN-TASTIC FAVORITES

Sports: Swimming

Movies: *Willy Wonka and the Chocolate Factory*, *Mary Poppins*, *The Matrix* trilogy

TV Shows: *South Park*, *The Daily Show*, *Martha*

Actors: Robert DeNiro, Vin Diesel, Marques Houston

Singers: Janet Jackson, Michael Jackson, Prince, Beyoncé, Brandy, Alanis Morissette, Chaka Khan, Jay-Z

Bands: Matchbox 20, Maroon 5

Hobbies: Cooking, drawing, making pottery

Board Game: Scrabble

Pastimes: Watching cooking shows on TV, shopping

Colors: Purple, red, pink, black

Food: Baked ziti, turkey

Down-Home Dinner: Grits and shrimp

Dessert: Crème brulée

Book: *Poems of Passion* by Ella Wheelers

Collections: Books of poetry, makeup

Secret Beauty Aid: Baby wipes —"They take off makeup in a snap."

GET IN TOUCH WITH RAVEN

Raven-Symoné
c/o Disney Channel
That's So Raven
3800 West Alameda Avenue
Burbank, CA 91505

Drake Bell

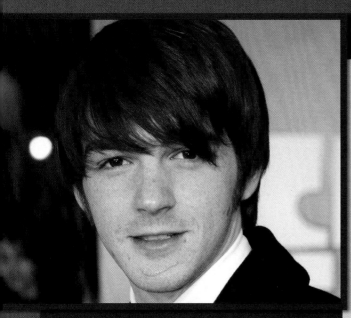

HEAD-TO-TOE STAX OF FAX

Name: Jared Drake Bell
Professional Name: Drake Bell
Nickname: The Drakester
Childhood Nickname: Boop
Birthday: June 27, 1986
Astro Sign: Cancer
Birthplace: Fountain Valley, CA
Hometown: Orange County, CA
Parents: Mom Robin Dodson (world-champion billiards player)
Siblings: Brothers Travis, Robert, Joey (all older), and sister Kelly (older)
Hair: Auburn
Eyes: Brown
Height: 5'10"
Pets: A dog named Halo and a cat named Natasha
Self-Description: "Impatient, unorganized, creative, and motivated"
Instruments: Guitar, drums, piano
Charity: Expedition Inspiration Fund for Breast Cancer Research

Performing has been Drake Bell's middle name since he got his first applause from family and friends. The singer/writer/musician/actor/comedian has been perfecting his craft from the day he was signed to his first agent! His best-known role was on Nickelodeon's *The Amanda Show*, where he and partner-in-fun Josh Peck made the audience of the hit show laugh and laugh! Drake and Josh's comic flare was so popular, the network developed their own show, *Drake and Josh*, which now is also a major must-see TV pick. On the series, Drake began highlighting his singing skills and he even wrote the show's theme song. In 2005, Drake released his first CD, *Telegraph*. Things were looking great, but as 2005 drew to a close, Drake was in a very serious car accident. He was stopped in his prized car, a 1966 Mustang, when another driver, who was speeding on the wrong side of the road, slammed into the side of Drake's car. Seriously injured, Drake was rushed to the hospital with a broken jaw and neck. He needed 1,500 stitches in his face, and his jaw was wired shut. However, by March 2006, a very thankful Drake was well enough to go back to work on *Drake and Josh* . . . and count his blessings that he is okay!

NOTABLE QUOTABLE
On His Home Decor

When he moved into his own apartment, Drake says, "I bought everything at the Salvation Army and Goodwill, and not one piece of furniture cost over $50, so I scored big-time. It's sort of neo-grandma."

GET IN TOUCH WITH DRAKE

Drake Bell
c/o Nickelodeon
Drake & Josh
2600 Colorado Avenue
Santa Monica, CA 90404

FUN-TASTIC FAVORITES

Vacation Place: Hawaii
TV Shows: *SpongeBob SquarePants, Curb Your Enthusiasm*
Movie: *School of Rock*
Actors: Benicio Del Toro, Brad Pitt, Kevin Spacey
Actress: Selma Blair
Bands: The Beatles, The Stray Cats
Performers: Paul McCartney, Brian Setzer
Car: 1957 Corvette
Family Dinner: Chicken enchilada casserole
Fast Food Restaurant: In-N-Out
Drink: Lemonade
Candy: Caramel, red Gummi Bears
Ice Cream: Cookies 'n' Cream and Rocky Road
Dessert: Crème brulée
Fashion Designer/Label: Diesel
Color: Orange
Book: *Catcher in the Rye* by J. D. Salinger
Author: Mark Twain
School Subject: History
Historical Era: 1950s –"because the styles were cool and Elvis was king!"

JoJo

HEAD-TO-TOE STAX OF FAX

Name: Joanna Noelle Levesque

Nickname: JoJo or Jo

Birthday: December 20, 1990

Astro Sign: Sagittarius

Birthplace: Foxborough, MA

Hometown: Foxborough, MA

Parents: JoJo's parents divorced when she was five years old and her mom, Diana, raised her. Her mom sang in her church choir and her father was a blues singer.

Hair: Brown

Eyes: Brown

Height: 5'4"

Boyfriend: Soccer star Freddie Adu

Pet: A dog named Sugarpie

Early Musical Influences: Whitney Houston, Etta James, Aretha Franklin, Ella Fitzgerald

First Professional Job: An episode of *Kids Say the Darnedest Things*

Number of Songs on Her iPod: "Twenty-five hundred — I mean, I don't listen to them all. But they're there!"

Places She Would Most Like to Go: Egypt and South Africa

Back when JoJo was a little girl of seven and better known as Joanna Levesque, she got her first taste of the spotlight. She appeared on Bill Cosby's TV show *Kids Say the Darnedest Things* and sang Aretha Franklin's "Respect." The audience was totally blown away — including Cosby. She didn't win the competition, but she did get a record deal and soon became the youngest artist to have a number one single when she released "Leave (Get Out)." Her career has taken off since then. In 2006 JoJo starred with Sara Paxton and Emma Roberts in the feature film *Aquamarine*. She also was in the 2006 film *RV* with Robin Williams.

36

FUN-TASTIC FAVORITES

Actor: Denzel Washington

Actress: Reese Witherspoon

Movie: *Crash*

Childhood Movies: *101 Dalmatians* and *The Little Mermaid* – JoJo loved the villains Cruella De Vil and Ursula!

Sports Team: New England Patriots

TV Show: "I don't really watch much TV, but *America's Next Top Model.*"

Solo Singers: Beyoncé, Kanye West, R. Kelly

Song: "Brown Sugar" by D'Angelo

Lyrics in One of Her Songs: "Poor kids pouring cold water in their cereal . . ." from "Keep On Keeping On."

Food: Macaroni and cheese

Candy: Snickers

Fast Food Restaurants: El Pollo Loco, Friendly's

Drink: Peppermint tea

Holiday: "I love Christmas – it is great because the family all comes together and celebrates each other, and that's really beautiful."

Vacation Spot: The Bahamas – the Atlantis Resort in Nassau

City: London

Clothes: Sundresses, jeans, and boots

Piece of Jewelry: A diamond cross necklace and a diamond-encrusted ring in the form of a *J*

Books: *Autobiography of Malcolm X*

Childhood Books: *Mother Goose* and *Harry Potter* series

School Subject: History

NOTABLE QUOTABLE
On Growing Up Poor

"My friends would go to the mall and the movies and I couldn't. I had hand-me-downs and shopped at Wal*Mart and K-Mart. . . . I lived in a middle-class area, but I was the poorest kid there, so it was hard. I lived in a one-bedroom apartment with my mom. I was just grateful that I didn't live on the street and I was never in a homeless shelter."

GET IN TOUCH WITH JOJO

JoJo
c/o *Aquamarine*
20th Century Fox
Home Entertainment
2121 Avenue of the Stars
Los Angeles, CA 90067

Chris Brown

HEAD-TO-TOE STAX OF FAX

Name: Christopher Brown

Birthday: May 5, 1989

Astro Sign: Taurus

Birthplace: Tappahannock, VA

Hometown: Tappahannock, VA

Parents: Mom Joyce Hawkins and dad Clinton Brown

Sibling: Sister Lytrell (older)

Hair: Brown

Eyes: Brown

Height: 6'1"

Early Musical Influences: Michael Jackson, Sam Cooke, Stevie Wonder, Donnie Hathaway, Bobbie Brown, New Edition, Marvin Gaye

Self-Description: "Outgoing, funny, charismatic, charming"

Chris burst onto the scene with the release of the single "Run It" from his debut CD, *Chris Brown*. The single zoomed to the top of the pop and R&B *Billboard* charts, and the CD itself opened at the number two spot on the *Billboard* albums chart. So, at age 16, the young singer from Virginia was already a superstar!

FUN-TASTIC FAVORITES

Best Gift Ever Received: A trampoline – "I've always wanted one!"

iPod Playlist: OutKast, R. Kelly, 50 Cent, Kanye West, Ciara

Song on His CD: "Winner"

Sports Teams: Miami Heat (NBA), Atlanta Falcons (NFL)

Sports: Basketball, football

Car: Black Range Rover – Chris hopes he will buy one as his first car! Chris would also love to own a Shelby Cobra.

School Subject: Math

Hobby: Drawing Japanese anime

Books: The *Harry Potter* series

Childhood Book: *Green Eggs and Ham* by Dr. Seuss

Food: Cheesecake

Homemade Meal: His grandma's chili

Snacks: Chocolate, Starbursts

Cities: Los Angeles, Miami, Atlanta

Designer/Label: Sean John

Holiday: Christmas

NOTABLE QUOTABLE
On His Pet Peeve

"I hate feet! I don't care if they're pretty or not — I just hate 'em!"

GET IN TOUCH WITH CHRIS

Chris Brown
c/o Sony Records
550 Madison Avenue
New York, NY 10022

Miley Cyrus

HEAD-TO-TOE STAX OF FAX

Name: Miley Cyrus
Nickname: Smiley
Birthday: November 23, 1992
Astro Sign: Sagittarius
Birthplace: Nashville, TN
Hometown: Nashville, TN
Parents: Tish and Billy Ray Cyrus
Siblings: Sisters Brandi and Noah, brothers Trace and Braison
Height: 5'2"
Hair: Brown
Eyes: Green-blue
Pets: Four dogs, five horses, two cats, and chickens
Best Advice Ever Gotten: "Treat people the way I want to be treated."
Instrument: Guitar

The daughter of country-rock superstar Billy Ray Cyrus, Miley has been dancing to the music since she was born! The Nashville-born teen loved going on stage with her dad when he performed and even appeared in some of her dad's TV projects. She had a recurring role in his series *Doc*, and by then knew she wanted to be in front of the cameras! Her family recently moved from Nashville to Los Angeles, and she and her dad signed on to work together again — this time for the Disney Channel's newest hit, *Hannah Montana*.

FUN-TASTIC FAVORITES

Sports: Cheerleading
TV Show: *Laguna Beach*
Movie: *Steel Magnolias*
Actress: Sandra Bullock
Food: Cookie dough
Fast Food Restaurant: In-N-Out
Ice Cream: Kona Chip
After-School Snack: Ramen noodles
Article of Clothing: Her Mickey Mouse sweat-shirt
School Subjects: Math, Astronomy
Book: *Don't Die, My Love*
Childhood Book: *Little Ballerina*
Author: Roald Dahl
Pastime: Braiding her horse's tail, writing music
Singers: Kelly Clarkson, Hilary Duff, Ashlee Simpson

GET IN TOUCH WITH MILEY

Miley Cyrus
c/o Disney Channel
Hannah Montana
3800 West Alameda Avenue
Burbank, CA 91505

NOTABLE QUOTABLE
On Reading

"I do like to read. Reading is kind of my thing after getting home from work. I don't really watch TV."

Jonas Brothers

NICHOLAS   JOSEPH   KEVIN

HEAD-TO-TOE STAX OF FAX

Name: Paul Kevin Jonas
Stage Name: Kevin Jonas
Birthday: November 5, 1987
Astro Sign: Scorpio
Birthplace: New Jersey
Hometown: Wyckoff, NJ
Brothers: Nicholas, Joseph, Frankie (all younger)
Pet: A dog named Cocoa
Self-Description: "Loving life, playing my music all the time"
Instrument: Guitar

FUN-TASTIC FAVORITES

Sports: Pole vault
TV Show: *Lost*
Movies: *About a Boy*, *Dead Poets Society*
Actor: James Dean
Singer: John Mayer
Car: Mini Cooper
Food: Ice cream! Especially rocky road
Fast Food Restaurant: McDonald's
After-School Snack: Bagel

"Music on Red Bull" is how eldest Jonas brother, Kevin, describes their music. Kevin and his two younger brothers, Joseph and Nicholas, exploded onto the music scene with their high-powered, energetic sound in early 2006. Their first single/video, "Mandy," climbed up into MTV's *TRL* Top Ten almost overnight, and then fans got a special bonus of two more "Mandy" videos that followed. The New Jersey brothers had a solid fan base for months before the release of their debut CD, *It's About Time,* because of Internet buzz. Those fans were quickly joined by others when the Jonas Brothers went on tour to schools and clubs across the country. The final word? These are brothers to watch!

GET IN TOUCH WITH JONAS BROTHERS

Kevin Jonas
Nick Jonas
Joseph Jonas
c/o Columbia Records
550 Madison Avenue
New York, NY 10022

HEAD-TO-TOE STAX OF FAX

Name: Joseph Adam Jonas

Birthday: August 15, 1989

Astro Sign: Leo

Birthplace: Arizona

Self-Description: "CRAZY! Ha-Ha – I just love to have fun!"

Fantasy Dream Place: Willy Wonka's chocolate factory

What Makes Him Laugh: Jim Carrey

What Makes Him Cry: When he sneezes

Dream Invention: "I would like to invent ice cream that never melts."

FUN-TASTIC FAVORITES

Sports: Baseball and Wiffleball

TV Shows: *Lost*, *The Office*, *Unwrapped*

Movie: *Liar, Liar*

Actor: Jim Carrey

Actress: Natalie Portman

Food: Power Bar

Drink: Gatorade

Candy: Tootsie Rolls

Ice Cream: Chocolate marshmallow

HEAD-TO-TOE STAX OF FAX

Name: Nicholas Jerry Jonas

Birthday: September 16, 1992

Astro Sign: Virgo

Birthplace: Dallas, TX

Self-Description: "I love to sing and play music. I love sports and I am very serious about everything I do in life."

Best Advice: "To live like you're at the bottom even if you are at the top."

What Makes Him Laugh: "My brothers"

What Makes Him Cry: "Onions"

FUN-TASTIC FAVORITES

Sports: Baseball

Sports Team: The NY Yankees

TV Shows: *Lost*, ESPN *SportsCenter*

Movies: *Finding Neverland*, *Better Off Dead*

Actor: Jake Long

Singer/Musician: Stevie Wonder

Car: Escalade

Food: Steak

Fast Food Restaurant: McDonald's

43

Aly & A.J.

A.J.   ALY

Name: Amanda Joy Michalka
Nickname: A.J.
Birthday: April 10, 1991
Astro Sign: Aries
Birthplace: Torrance, CA
Hometown: Los Angeles, CA
Height: 5'5¼"
Pets: Two Australian cattle dog/ German shepherd mix – Saint and Bandit
Self-Description: "Positive outlook on life; goal oriented and organized without taking the fun out of life."

Alyson (Aly) and Amanda (A.J.) Michalka are not only sisters but the California beauties are best friends, too. They have been performing together nearly all their lives. Aly is best known for costarring in the hit Disney channel series *Phil of the Future*. A.J. has also appeared in various TV roles, but it is music that is putting the sisters in the limelight right now. They released their debut CD, *Into the Rush*, in 2005 — they wrote or cowrote twelve of the songs on the CD. A.J. and Aly spent most of 2005 and much of 2006 touring in support of the CD — taking time off only to film their Disney Channel TV movie, *Cow Belles*. There is also talk about a possible new Disney Channel sitcom series for Aly and A.J. called *Havensham Hall*.

HEAD-TO-TOE STAX OF FAX

Name: Alyson Renae Michalka
Nickname: Aly
Birthday: March 25, 1989
Astro Sign: Aries
Birthplace: Torrance, CA
Hometown: Los Angeles, CA
Parents: Mark and Carrie Michalka
Height: 5'6"
Instrument: Guitar, piano

FUN-TASTIC FAVORITES

Sports: Horseback riding

Actor: Johnny Depp

Actress: Cate Blanchett

Band: Switchfoot, The Jonas Brothers

Singers: John Mayer, Sting, Seal

Car: Range Rover

Candy: Ring Pops of all flavors

Food: Sushi

Ice Cream: Chocolate chip cookie dough

After-School Snack: Peanut butter and celery

Color: Purple

Book: The *Artemis Fowl* series

ALY

NOTABLE QUOTABLE
On What They Never Leave Home Without

"A.J. and I always bring our two teddy bears, Winthrop and Tuffy [on the road with us]. We also bring photos of our doggies. Luckily we've never misplaced them. If we did, we would freak!"

FUN-TASTIC FAVORITES

Food: Sushi, pasta

Candy: Ring Pops and Pop Rocks

TV Shows: *That '70s Show*, *The O.C.*

Actresses: Naomi Watts, Cate Blanchett

Band: Nickelback, The Jonas Brothers

Singers: Seal, John Mayer, Sting, Michelle Branch

Pastimes: Drawing, fashion design, sewing

Book Series: *Lemony Snickett's Series of Unfortunate Events* and *Artemis Fowl*

Colors: Orange, cranberry, black

School Subjects: English and History

A.J.

NOTABLE QUOTABLE
On Her Silliest New Year's Resolution

"I once promised to stay away from candy. That didn't last too long."

GET IN TOUCH WITH ALY & A.J.

Aly & A.J. Michalka
Cow Belles
c/o Disney Channel
3800 West Alameda Avenue
Burbank, CA 91505

Omarion

HEAD-TO-TOE STAX OF FAX

Name: Omari Ishmael Grandberry
Nickname: O
Stage Name: Omarion
Birthday: November 12, 1984
Astro Sign: Scorpio
Birthplace: Los Angeles, CA
Hometown: Los Angeles, CA
Parents: Mom Leslie Burrell, dad Trent Grandberry
Siblings: Sisters Arielle, Amira, Kera, brothers O'Ryan, Tymon, Ukil (all younger)
Pets: Two American terriers (pit bulls) named Peaches and Flimflame
Childhood Pet: A German shepherd named Dusty
Hair: Brown
Eyes: Brown
Height: 5'7"
Self-Description As Child: "Cute and always into stuff."
Best Friend: His uncle and manager, Chris Stokes – Chris is married to Omarion's aunt Monyee.
Language Studied In School: Spanish

When Omarion was a little boy growing up in the inner city of Los Angeles, music was always with him. Though his parents, Leslie and Trent, weren't together – Omarion and his mom lived with his grandmother, Nana – he was surrounded by lots of love, too. Even today, Omarion remembers his father introducing him to the music of Marvin Gaye and Earth, Wind & Fire, and the young singer says their influence is still with him. When Omarion was 16, he burst onto the scene with the multiplatinum group B2K. When the group split up four years later, Omarion didn't miss a beat – he went into the studio to record his debut solo CD, O, lined up movie after movie, and even wrote an autobiography, also titled O.

FUN-TASTIC FAVORITES

Sports: Basketball, football
Sports Star: Kobe Bryant
Sports Team: Los Angeles Lakers
TV Shows: *Teen Titans*, *Dragon Balls 2*, *Family Matters*, *The Martin Lawrence Show* (all-time fave!)
Movies: *You Got Served*, *Beverly Hills Cop*, *Bad Boys*, *Gladiator*, *Remember the Titans*, *Lord of the Rings* trilogy, *Braveheart*, *The Matrix*, *The Five Heartbeats*
Singers: Tupac, Kim Burrell, Eric Dawkins, Tonex
Dinner: Jambalaya
Breakfast: Grand Slam Slugger breakfast at Denny's
Fast Food: Onion rings
Candy: Gummi Bears
Dessert: Ice cream
Gum: Big Red
Historical Figures: Malcolm X, Martin Luther King Jr.
Animal: Dog
Car: Hummer
Article of Clothing: Bandannas

NOTABLE QUOTABLE
On Telling a Bad Joke

"A bad joke — is there any other kind?
Man #1: Knock. Knock.
Man #2: Get away from my door."

GET IN TOUCH WITH OMARION

Omarion
c/o Sony Music/Epic
550 Madison Avenue
New York, NY 10022

Teddy Geiger

HEAD-TO-TOE STAX OF FAX

Name: John Theodore Geiger II
Nickname: Teddy
Stage Name: Teddy Geiger
Birthday: September 16, 1988
Astro Sign: Virgo
Birthplace: Buffalo, NY
Hometown: Pittsford, NY
Parents: John and Lorilyn
Siblings: Brother A.J., sister Rachel (both younger)
Hair: Brown
Eyes: Blue
Height: 5'11"
Pet: Dog named Buddy
Instruments: Guitar, piano
Best Friend: His cousin Torre Catalano

FUN-TASTIC FAVORITES

Movie: *Rushmore*
Book: *Ender's Game* by Orson Scott Card
Pastime: Hanging out with friends and playing music
Sandwich: Philly cheese steaks
Drink: Energy drinks
Clothes: T-shirts and jeans
Singer: Dave Matthews
Bands: Ben Folds Five, Weezer
CD: *Whatever & Ever Amen* by Ben Folds Five

Born in Buffalo, New York, Teddy began playing the guitar when he was only eight years old. Even back then, the talented young musician, who is now 18, knew what he wanted out of life. When he was 15, Teddy entered the VH1 reality show *In Search of the Partridge Family*. Though Teddy didn't win the competition to be the "new" Keith Partridge, legendary music producer Billy Mann noticed him. That introduction was the beginning of Teddy's dream come true — a CD, *Underage Thinking*; a role on a TV series, *Love Monkey*; and a single, "For You I Will (Confidence)"; and hitting the top of the charts.

GET IN TOUCH WITH TEDDY

Teddy Geiger
c/o Columbia Records
550 Madison Avenue
New York, NY 10022